For Gina and Catherine - S.G.

This edition published in 1998 by Hodder Children's Book
a division of Hodder Headline plc,
338 Euston Road, London NW1 3BH

10 9 8 7 6 5 4 3 2

The rights of Sally Grindley to be identified as author
of the text of this work, and of Susan Varley to be
identified as the illustrator of this work
has been asserted by them in accordance with the
Copyright, Design and Patents Act 1998

A Catalogue record for this book is available from the British Library

ISBN 0 340 698438

First published in Great Britain in 1996
by Andersen Press Ltd

Printed in Hong Kong

Why is the Sky Blue?

Written by Sally Grindley

Illustrated by Susan Varley

Hodder
Children's
Books

A division of Hodder Headline plc

Rabbit and Donkey lived in the same field.
Donkey spent his days in the corner nodding
his head wisely and chewing on grass.

Rabbit popped up all over the place. His burrow
had many openings, and he used them all.

Donkey was very old and knew a lot of things.

"I know why trees lose their leaves, and how spiders spin their webs, and why the sky is blue," he told anyone who would listen.

Rabbit was very young and wanted to learn.

"I want to learn everything there is to learn," said Rabbit.

"I will teach you what I know," said Donkey, "which is a lot."

"Goody," said Rabbit. "Yes, please."

And he jumped and he ran and he rolled and he bounced across the field and back again.

"I will teach you what I know," said Donkey, "which is a lot. But I can only teach you if you sit still and listen."

"I will sit still," said Rabbit. "I will sit still and listen."

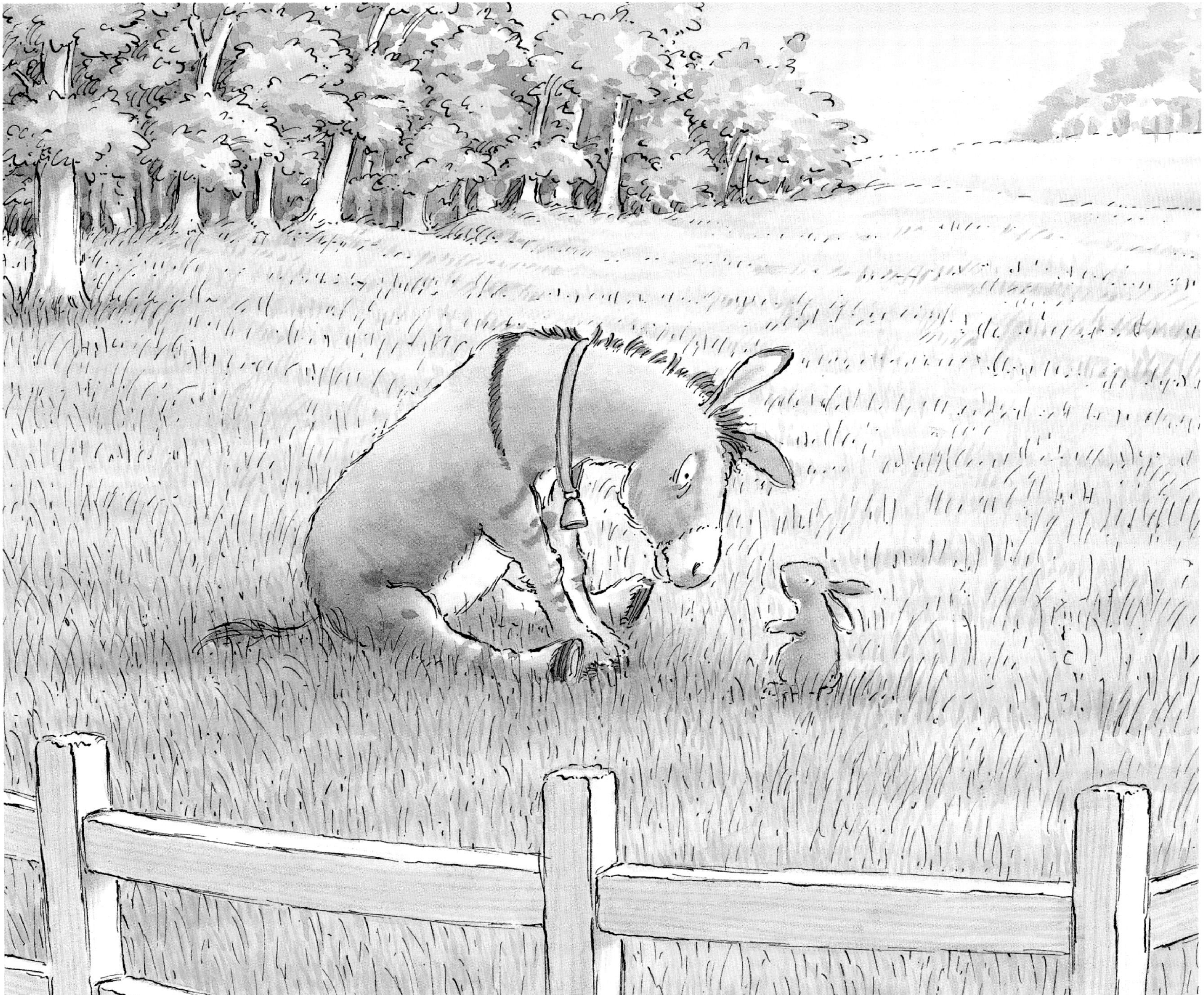

Donkey began. "I am going to tell you why the sky is blue."

"Goody," said Rabbit. "I really want to know why the sky is blue."

But before Donkey had got very far, Rabbit wanted to know why the earth is brown. And before he had got any further, Rabbit was jumping around the field pointing at yellow flowers and red berries and white butterflies.

Donkey chewed crossly on a piece of grass and waited... and waited. When at last he came back, Rabbit said eagerly, "I found out why berries are red. Shall I tell you why?"

"I know already," said Donkey. "And now it is time for my sleep."

"Oh, but I missed why the sky is blue," said Rabbit. "And I really want to know why. Can I come back tomorrow and have another lesson?"

"I can only teach you if you sit still and listen," said Donkey.

"I will sit still," said Rabbit. "I will sit still and I will listen."

"Then tomorrow I will teach you what I know," said Donkey, "which is a lot."

Rabbit leapt in the air in excitement and ran and rolled and bounced across the field all the way home to tea.

The next day, Donkey began again to tell Rabbit why the sky is blue. But before Donkey had got very far, Rabbit wanted to know about the sun and the moon and the stars. And before he had got any further, Rabbit was rushing around pointing at the clouds and the giant foxes and owls he could see amongst them.

Donkey chewed crossly on a piece of grass and waited… and waited.

When at last he came back, Rabbit said eagerly, "Sometimes you can see the moon even when the sun is out."

"I know that," said Donkey. "And now it is time for my sleep."

"Oh, but I missed why the sky is blue, again," said Rabbit. "And I really want to know why. Can I come back tomorrow and have another lesson?"

"One last time," said Donkey. "But I can only teach you if you sit still and listen."

"I will sit still," said Rabbit. "I will sit still and listen."

"Then I will teach you what I know," said Donkey, "which is a lot."

Rabbit leapt in the air in excitement…

…and ran…

…and rolled…

…and bounced…
…across the field all the way home to tea.

The next day, Donkey began again to tell Rabbit why the sky is blue, but before he had got very far Rabbit wanted to know why birds could fly and he couldn't. And before he had got any further, Rabbit was running up a slope and leaping off it making bird noises and flapping his paws.

Donkey chewed crossly on a piece of grass and waited… and waited.

Rabbit didn't come back.

Donkey settled down for his sleep and then looked across the field. He couldn't see Rabbit anywhere. He began to worry.

"He's young," he said to himself. "He might have got into trouble. I'd better go and find him."

He set off slowly across the field. After a few steps he came to a clump of yellow flowers. He looked amongst them for Rabbit. Rabbit wasn't there, but he watched the bees collecting pollen from the flower-heads.

"It sticks to their legs," he said to himself. "I never noticed that before."

He set off again, more quickly this
time, and as he trotted along he looked
at the sky and saw woolly sheep
amongst the clouds.

"It's a long time since I played that game," he smiled to himself.

He came to the top of the slope Rabbit had run down.
He looked around to make sure no one was watching, then he
began to gallop. When he reached the bottom he galloped on,
enjoying the wind tugging at his ears and ruffling his coat.

"It's a long time since I felt that feeling," he laughed to himself.

And then he saw Rabbit, sitting quite still in the middle
of a gorse bush.

"Shhh," said Rabbit when he saw Donkey.

"I was worried about you," whispered Donkey.
"What are you doing?"

"I'm counting the spots on ladybirds," said Rabbit.
"Did you know that some have more spots than others?"

"No," said Donkey, in amazement, "I didn't know that.
I know a lot of things but I didn't know that. Let me see."

Rabbit and Donkey looked together. They sat still and counted spots until Rabbit began to yawn.

"Donkey," said Rabbit, "can you lift me out of here? I'm stuck."

Donkey smiled. "Hang on to my ears then," he said, lowering his head so that Rabbit could reach. He pulled him out and set him on the ground.

"Come," said Donkey, "I'll take you back home. Today you have taught me something new. Tomorrow I will teach you why the sky is blue."

"But I know why the sky is blue," said Rabbit.

"You do?" said Donkey.

"It's because that was the only colour left in the paintbox," said Rabbit.

Donkey smiled. Donkey laughed. Donkey cheered and kicked his legs in the air. Then he jumped and he ran and he rolled and he bounced, across the field and back again.

"That's the funniest thing I've heard for a long time," said Donkey. "Climb on my back and I'll carry you, but you must sit still."

"Donkey," said Rabbit. "Why *is* the sky blue?"

Donkey began to tell Rabbit about sunlight and the dust in the air, but before he had got very far, Rabbit had fallen asleep. Donkey smiled to himself.

"Never mind," he said. "It can wait until morning."